Veronica

∂ THE SHOW-OFF

Veronica
❧ THE SHOW-OFF

NANCY K. ROBINSON

FOUR WINDS PRESS
Macmillan Publishing Company
New York

Collier Macmillan Publishers
London

Macmillan Publishing Company
866 Third Avenue, New York, NY 10022
Collier Macmillan Canada, Inc.

Printed in the United States of America

The text of this book is set in 12 pt. Primer.

10 9 8 7 6 5 4 3

Library of Congress Cataloging in Publication Data

Robinson, Nancy K.
  Veronica, the show-off.

  Summary: Although lonely and desperately in need of
friends, Veronica overwhelms her new classmates with her
outrageous behaviour.
  [1. Behavior—Fiction. 2. Friendship—Fiction] 1. Title.
PZ7.R56754Ve 1985   [Fic]   85-4483
ISBN 0-02-777360-4

TO BEV . . .
for all the celebrations!

Veronica

❧ THE SHOW-OFF

Veronica's
❧ Horse

Veronica looked around the classroom. She had
nothing to do. She had already finished her homework for the next day.

Veronica reached forward and tapped Kimberly
on the shoulder. Ever since her first day at Maxton
Academy, Veronica had wanted to be friends with
Kimberly Watson.

"Kimberly," she whispered. But Kimberly did
not seem to hear her. Kimberly was doing her
math homework. Veronica knew that Kimberly
had horseback lessons every afternoon right after
school and was supposed to get all her homework
done in the free period before lunch.

Veronica waited a few seconds and tapped
again, but Kimberly still didn't seem to notice.

Veronica poked Kimberly in the back.

"What?" Kimberly whirled around and stared
at Veronica.

"I have a sweater just like yours at home," said Veronica. Kimberly was wearing a light blue sweater with a snowflake design around the collar. It was the prettiest sweater Veronica had ever seen.

"That's impossible," said Kimberly. "My mother knitted it for me. It's an original design."

"So's mine," said Veronica.

Kimberly shrugged and turned back to her work.

"I'll wear mine tomorrow," Veronica whispered. She had to poke Kimberly again. "I said, I'll wear mine tomorrow. Then we can be twins."

"Whatever you say, Veronica." Kimberly looked across the aisle at Amy. Amy giggled.

"Unless it's at the cleaner's," Veronica went on. "Now that I think of it, it might be at the cleaner's."

Veronica did not have a light blue sweater with a snowflake design around the collar. She was only trying to be friendly. She couldn't understand why no one at her new school was trying to be friendly back.

She studied the back of Kimberly's head. Kimberly was twirling a piece of her long blond hair around her finger. Then she put it in her mouth and chewed on it.

Maybe she's shy! Veronica knew that shy people often appear to be unfriendly. *I'll give her another chance.*

At lunch time Veronica found a seat right across from Kimberly and Amy. The tuna casserole reminded Veronica of her cat, so she told them all about her rare cat named Gulliver who was about to be offered a job in a cat food commercial.

Veronica couldn't remember if she had already told them she had two color TV sets, so she told them again—just to be sure.

Every time Veronica said, "That reminds me, did I tell you about . . ." Amy looked up at the ceiling and groaned. Veronica thought she probably had a stomachache. But Kimberly never said a word. She never even looked up from her tray.

That proves it! Veronica told herself. *She definitely is shy.*

Then Veronica got a wonderful idea. All she had to do was to talk about the subject that interested Kimberly most. Then Kimberly wouldn't feel so shy.

"By the way, Kimberly," said Veronica. "Did I ever tell you about my horse?"

Kimberly looked up from her tray. "What horse?" she asked. Kimberly sounded interested.

"Oh, the horse I almost got for my birthday," said Veronica.

Amy groaned very loudly. Veronica wondered if she ought to see the school nurse.

"All right, Veronica," Kimberly sighed. "Tell me about the horse you *almost* got for your birthday."

Veronica took a deep breath. "Well, you won't believe this, but, you see, my grandfather wanted to buy me my own private horse—a thorough-bredded horse. He had this particular horse in mind—a world-famous thoroughbredded horse, but I'm not allowed to say his name. You would know him the minute I said his name—"

"Why can't you say his name?" Amy asked.

"—so anyway," Veronica went on. "My mother said she didn't think it was fair to a horse to keep him in the city—"

"Were you going to keep him in your apartment?" Amy asked.

"Well, no . . ." said Veronica. She thought Amy was rude to keep interrupting like this. ". . . although our apartment *is* quite big. So anyway, we had this nice stable all lined up for this extremely expensive world-famous horse and then it turned out that someone else wanted this horse—whose name I can't mention. I can't mention the horse's name and I can't mention this person's name because he is terribly famous and well known and lives in California on acres and acres because of being a big movie star and owning this enormous ranch where horses can roam free . . ."

Veronica thought "roam free" sounded very nice. She was about to go on when she noticed she was sitting all by herself at the table. Kimberly and Amy were already at the other end of the lunchroom, putting their trays on the counter.

Veronica didn't think it was polite of Kimberly and Amy to leave the table without saying "Excuse me."

And, if Kimberly isn't interested in horses, what is she interested in? Veronica wondered.

After lunch everyone went out to a playing field for recess. The field had a fence all around it made of tall iron bars. Only Maxton Academy kids were allowed to play there. There was a fancy iron gate that was always locked. Sometimes Veronica wished that someone from her old public school would just happen to pass by and see her running around in a private park!

During recess Veronica decided it was time to help Kimberly get over her shyness. She looked all over for Kimberly.

At last she saw her. Kimberly was standing with Amy under one of the big trees. Kimberly was whispering in Amy's ear. At the same time she was keeping an eye on Jacob, who was circling around them.

Suddenly Jacob rushed forward and dropped a bunch of autumn leaves on Kimberly's head. Then he ran around to the other side of the tree.

"Jacob!" Kimberly yelled. "You're going to get it!" Kimberly and Amy began piling leaves together on the ground. Veronica went over and tried to help them.

"Hold him, Kimberly!" Amy shouted. Kimberly grabbed Jacob and held him while Amy stuffed leaves down his jacket.

Two other boys ran over to help Jacob. Soon everybody was throwing leaves.

Veronica stood in the middle. She was hoping to get hit with some leaves. But the fight went on around her—almost as if she weren't there.

Now Amy was holding Jacob by the sleeve of his jacket while Kimberly poured leaves on top of his head. Jacob pulled his arms out of his jacket and ran. Amy was still holding his jacket. Kimberly collapsed on a pile of leaves and lay there giggling.

Veronica decided that this was *not* a good time to help Kimberly get over her shyness.

Hilary 🦋

Veronica waited at the bus stop. There was only one girl in Veronica's class who took the same bus home. Her name was Hilary. Veronica and Hilary lived on the other side of town; everyone else lived near the school.

Veronica had decided that it would not be worth her time trying to make friends with Hilary. Hilary didn't seem to have any friends. She wouldn't be able to do Veronica much good.

Hilary was pretty. She had dark curly hair pulled up in a bunch on top of her head. Her face was so small and delicate she looked like an old-fashioned doll.

Veronica was big for her age and did not trust little cute people.

Hilary was wearing patent leather party shoes and short white socks folded at the ankle.

No one at Maxton Academy wore white socks folded at the ankle. Everyone wore high white socks and white sneakers that always looked brand-new.

No wonder she doesn't have any friends, Veronica thought.

But the worst thing about Hilary was that she had a nervous twitch. Every once in a while Hilary looked up and blinked her eyes very fast. Veronica wished Hilary wouldn't do that. It really scared her.

The bus was crowded. Veronica ran to get a seat. She sat down right on top of a lady's hand. The lady was trying to save that seat for a friend.

"You're not allowed to save seats," Veronica explained to the lady. "It's a public bus."

Veronica made herself comfortable and looked around for Hilary.

Hilary never sat down on the bus. She usually held on to a pole and stared out the window. Today she was standing right next to the bus driver.

Veronica was watching her when she saw Hilary's eyes begin to flutter. Veronica looked away quickly. *How awful!* she thought.

When she was sure that Hilary's eyes had stopped fluttering, Veronica turned back and stared at Hilary's socks. *How babyish. How can anyone wear socks like that?*

Hilary carried a flowered shopping bag instead of a book bag. That really disgusted Veronica. *Unbelievable!* she told herself.

Then Veronica noticed a book sticking out of Hilary's shopping bag. It was a dark red book. It wasn't a schoolbook. In fact, it looked very much like a Polly Winkler Mystery Story.

Veronica loved Polly Winkler Mystery Stories. She had read every single one, except the latest one.

And the only reason she hadn't read the newest Polly Winkler was that some girl named Melody Hicks had taken it out of her neighborhood library. Veronica knew the name of the girl who had the book because she had peeked over the librarian's shoulder at the card. And every day Veronica had stopped by the library on her way home to see if the book was back.

The book was due back today! Veronica couldn't wait to get her hands on it. It was called *The Clue in the Whispering Willow*, and Veronica thought it sounded terrific.

Veronica stared at the dark red book in Hilary's shopping bag. *It must be a Polly Winkler!* she thought.

Finally she couldn't stand it another minute.

10

She jumped up and went over to Hilary. She hung on to the same pole.

"By any chance," Veronica said, "is that a Polly Winkler Mystery Story?" Veronica spoke in her quietest voice. She didn't want to frighten Hilary and start her blinking.

Hilary didn't blink. She smiled right at Veronica. Veronica was surprised that someone with such a tiny mouth could smile such a big smile.

"Why, yes it is," said Hilary. "It *is* a Polly Winkler."

"I knew it!" shouted Veronica. "I just knew it! Which one?"

"The Secret in the Haunted Canyon," said Hilary.

"Oh no! You must be kidding. You're only up to *that?* I read it months ago. I read the whole thing in one night. But, of course, I'm a terribly fast reader." Veronica shook her head sadly. "I just can't believe you're only on that one. I've read every single one—some I've read twice."

"This is my first one," said Hilary. She was still smiling. "It belongs to my older sister."

"You mean you didn't read *The Mystery at Sandy Point?"*

Hilary shook her head.

"Well, what about *When the Clock Struck Twelve?*"

"Nope," said Hilary. Veronica could hardly believe her ears.

"You've got to!" screeched Veronica. "You'll love it!"

Hilary's eyes began to flutter. Veronica caught her breath. She suddenly realized she was standing in the middle of a public bus talking to someone with a nervous twitch.

She looked around at the people on the bus. Had anyone noticed? She looked at Hilary again. Suddenly Veronica didn't care what anyone was thinking. It seemed far more important that Hilary read the right Polly Winklers. She simply had to.

"Look," said Veronica, "I'll tell you what. I'll take you to the library right now and help you pick out a whole bunch of Polly Winklers. Then I'll show you what order to read them in. You've got to read them in a certain order. And, whatever you do, do not read *The CB Mystery*. It sounds terrific, but it's just terrible."

"I can't go to the library today," said Hilary. "What about tomorrow?"

Veronica was disappointed. She didn't like to wait for anything.

"Why not? she demanded. "Why can't you go to the library today?"

"I've got a lesson," said Hilary.

Veronica looked Hilary up and down.

"Ballet?" she asked.

Hilary shook her head. Veronica looked at Hilary's small hands and tiny fingers.

"Piano?" she asked doubtfully.

Hilary shook her head again and started walking toward the back of the bus. "I've got to get off at the next stop," she said.

Veronica followed her to the bus door. When the bus stopped, Veronica grabbed Hilary's arm.

"Well, what kind of lesson is it?" Veronica asked crossly.

"Karate," Hilary whispered, and she stepped down off the bus.

Story Hour 🐛

The children's room of the library was crowded.
Every seat was taken. Some little kids were hopping around in the aisles. They were waiting for
the afternoon story hour.

Veronica looked all over Miss Markham's desk.
The librarian had promised to hold *The Clue in
the Whispering Willow* for her.

Because I'm her best customer, Veronica thought
proudly. *I'm probably her favorite reader, too.*

But Veronica didn't see the book. "Where is it?"
she asked. "Where's my book?"

Miss Markham looked up. "Oh, dear," she said.
"Oh, Veronica, I'm afraid I've got bad news for
you."

"Yes, but where's the book?" Veronica figured
she could hear the bad news later.

"Unfortunately," said Miss Markham, "it's been
renewed."

14

"I don't get it," said Veronica.

"Well, the girl who had it wasn't finished, so I let it go out again."

"I still don't get it," said Veronica. Her face felt stiff. "She can't have it. She's already had it two weeks."

But the librarian wasn't paying attention. She was looking nervously at two little kids who were chasing each other around the picture-book shelves.

"Quiet down, Jeremy," she called. "Find something to look at, Ruthie. The Story Lady will be here any minute now."

"I just have to hit her back," Jeremy called.

Miss Markham sighed and turned back to Veronica. When she saw Veronica's face, she got a shock. Veronica's face looked as if it had turned into stone. She was staring at Miss Markham, but she didn't seem to see her.

"Maybe she'll bring it back early." Miss Markham tried to sound cheerful. She knew how Veronica felt. When Miss Markham was Veronica's age, she had loved books. She knew how it felt to be desperate for a certain book. "Now, Veronica, why don't you just find yourself another book in the meantime."

"I'm not the least bit interested in another book," Veronica said. "You promised to hold that book for me and that's the only book I want."

"Oh, Veronica, I *am* sorry," said Miss Markham. "But I'm afraid there is nothing I can do."

"Yes there is," said Veronica fiercely. "You can call that dumb Melody Hicks and tell her to get the book back right this minute." Veronica didn't know Melody Hicks, but if Melody Hicks couldn't finish a Polly Winkler in two whole weeks, she *must* be dumb.

"Sh-h-h, Veronica, please keep your voice down," said Miss Markham.

"My voice *is* down!" Veronica shouted. "You don't understand. I've got to have that book. I can't wait for a . . . a . . . Slow Reader!"

"That's quite enough." Miss Markham spoke in a low voice. Veronica could tell she was angry. "You're not the only one who uses this library, Veronica, and if you cannot control yourself, you will have to leave."

Veronica suddenly remembered Hilary and the Polly Winkler reading program she was planning for her. Right at that moment Veronica decided to sign out every Polly Winkler in the library.

"Well, Veronica?" Miss Markham was waiting. "Are you ready to behave yourself?"

Veronica bit her lip and looked down at the floor. She nodded. Then she ran over to the Polly Winkler bookshelf.

Veronica couldn't believe her eyes. There were exactly two Polly Winklers left on the shelf. One was *The Secret in the Haunted Canyon* (Hilary already had that one), and the other was *The CB Mystery* (a terrible book!).

"Where are they?" shrieked Veronica. "They're all gone!"

Miss Markham came running over. The two little kids who had been chasing each other came, too. They wanted to see what was going on.

"Why is that girl screaming?" Ruthie asked Jeremy.

"Just a minute," said Jeremy. "I'll tell you." The little boy went and stood right in front of Veronica. He stared up at her. He looked at Veronica's face, which was now almost purple, and he looked down at Veronica's fists, which were white at the knuckles.

"She is angry," he said to the little girl.

When Veronica started yelling again, the little

girl covered her ears, but the little boy just stood there. He didn't seem to be scared, just interested.

"Just look!" Veronica screamed at Miss Markham. "They've been stolen!"

"Don't be silly," said Miss Markham. "They've been signed out."

"By who?" Veronica glared at Miss Markham. Then a terrible thought came to her. "Don't tell me," she said slowly. "I bet I know who it was. It was that stupid Melody, right?"

"Well, as a matter of fact . . . " Miss Markham began.

"I knew it!" Veronica shouted. "Melody Hicks is ruining everything. And it's all your fault for letting kids like her use the library. I'll bet Melody Hicks can't even read. I'll bet her mother has to read it out loud to her, one page every night and . . . and . . . and I'll bet Melody Hicks is the one who crayons all over the back page and . . . " Veronica was running out of terrible things to say about Melody Hicks.

The little boy nodded wisely. He turned to the little girl, who uncovered her ears to hear his report.

"She is angry," he said. He took a deep breath. "She is angry because this girl Melody crayoned

18

all over her book and tore out the pages and stuffed it down the garbage pail."

"That's terrible," said Ruthie.

Jeremy turned to Veronica and waited for her to go on. "Go ahead," he whispered. "Then what did she do?"

Veronica stared at the little boy. He had dark skin and curly black hair. He was looking up at her with big serious eyes.

Veronica's eyes began to sting. Her chest felt like it was going to burst. She had to get out of the library without crying.

"I just want you to know that I think you are a t-t-terrible librarian," she told Miss Markham. "You promised to hold *The Clue in the W-W-Willowing Whisper* for me and you didn't. You lied!"

Miss Markham no longer looked angry. She looked sad. But Veronica couldn't stop herself. It had been nice being Miss Markham's favorite reader, but now it was too late.

"I think you are the worst librarian in the whole w-w-world and you'll be sorry. I'm taking my business elsewhere."

Veronica turned and marched out of the library.

"Where is that girl going?" Ruthie asked.

"She's going to the supermarket," said Jeremy.

The Mysterious Melody &

Veronica hated Melody Hicks. She didn't know her. She had never met her. But she hated her more than anyone in the world.

She made me act like that, Veronica told herself.

Veronica was sitting in the kitchen with her mother. He mother was getting ready for a dinner party. She was filling celery stalks with a special cheese dip.

"Stop sulking, Veronica," her mother said.

"I'm not sulking," said Veronica. "It's my regular face."

"Your face looks horrid when you scrunch it up like that," her mother said. "I'm expecting the Stanfords for dinner. I want them to see how pretty my little girl is."

Veronica's mother was very pretty. She was tall and thin. She dressed like a fashion model. She had dark shiny hair that she wore long and tucked back behind her ears.

20

Veronica wore her hair the same way. Veronica and her mother went to the same hairdresser. His name was Peter. Peter also cut the hair of the Countess Anne Marie du Bellay.

Only last week the countess's picture had been on the society page of the newspaper. She was skiing in Switzerland. She was wearing sunglasses on top of her head.

Veronica cut out the picture and brought it to school. She wore sunglasses on top of her head, too.

"We almost bump into each other at the hairdresser," Veronica told everybody. "It's almost like being related." She sighed.

But no one seemed interested. "I never even heard of her," Amy had said.

Veronica took a piece of celery and cheese. Her mother took the platter and put it on top of the refrigerator.

"That's enough, Veronica," she said. "We really must watch our waistline. Now go put on the dress your father sent you from Mexico."

Veronica suddenly remembered something. "Mom," she said. "Isn't Daddy coming this weekend?"

Veronica's parents had been divorced when she was six years old. Her father lived in California. Veronica hadn't seen him since the summer. "Well, isn't he coming?" she asked.

"I believe he is," her mother said. She was sprinkling paprika over some stuffed mushrooms.

"You mean he's flying in from the coast?" Veronica was thrilled. And she loved to say "flying in from the coast." It sounded so glamorous.

"Well, yes," her mother said. "As a matter of fact, he called last night. He sends you his love."

"His love?" Veronica stared at her mother. "Isn't he going to see me?"

"Oh, dear." Veronica's mother turned around. "I probably shouldn't have said anything. You see, darling, he's got a terribly full schedule this weekend. He won't have a free second."

Veronica was sure her mother had gotten the story wrong. How could her father be in the same city and not want to see her? *Not want to see me? Me, Veronica?*

"Oh, Veronica, please don't look so unhappy," her mother said. "I'm sure he'll see you the next time."

"I'm not the least bit unhappy." Veronica carefully tucked her hair behind her ears. "Besides,

I've got a million things to do this weekend. I'm awfully busy myself."

"How cute," her mother said.

Veronica watched her mother put little black olives around the platter of mushrooms.

"How's school?" her mother asked.

"Umph," said Veronica.

"Please don't grunt, Veronica," her mother said. "It's so unattractive. And how's the little Watson girl?"

Veronica's mother was always asking about Kimberly Watson. She was interested in Kimberly because Kimberly's father was always giving money to good causes. Last year he had given a whole bunch of money to The Friends of Symphony Hall. Veronica's mother was on that committee.

Veronica grunted again. She didn't want to think about Kimberly. She was too busy hating Melody Hicks.

If only she knew what Melody looked like, how old she was, what school she went to. If only she knew how Melody Hicks acted. Then she would be able to hate her even more.

La Show-off 🚲

"It's probably not even her real name," Veronica said to Hilary on the bus the next morning. She had told Hilary all about Melody Hicks and the missing books—"the mysterious disappearance," as she liked to call it. That's what Polly Winkler would have called it.

And Hilary had told Veronica how much she had liked *The Secret in the Haunted Canyon*. "I finished the whole thing last night—under the covers with a flashlight."

"I read everything in one night," Veronica said. But she felt proud that Hilary had liked the Polly Winkler so much. Veronica felt as if she had written it herself.

"Believe me," said Veronica. "Something fishy is going on at that library. I wouldn't be the least bit surprised if it was *smugglers!*"

"Wow!" said Hilary. "What are smugglers?"

"Well, you would know immediately if you read more Polly Winklers," said Veronica.

Veronica didn't really know what a smuggler was. She figured it was a special kind of thief. But a smuggler sounded more glamorous. More dangerous, too.

"You think Melody Hicks is a criminal?" Hilary asked.

"Oh, probably part of a gang," said Veronica. "Miss Markham doesn't suspect a thing."

Veronica noticed that Hilary was wearing pink socks today—little pink party socks with lace around the cuffs.

"Oh, Hilary, I meant to ask. How was your karate lesson?" she asked staring down at the socks.

"Good," said Hilary.

"Are you, by any chance, a black belt?" Veronica knew that black belts went around smashing boards in two.

"No, I'm a green belt," said Hilary.

"Is that better?" Veronica asked.

"Are you kidding? Of course not," said Hilary. "But it's pretty good for my age."

Veronica decided she would never take karate lessons unless she could be a black belt.

"Well, are we going to the library today to *investigate?*" Hilary asked. She shivered with excitement.

"No!" said Veronica. "I mean, I don't think it's a good idea to return to the scene of the crime right away." Veronica couldn't face Miss Markham after what happened yesterday.

"Oh," said Hilary. "Well, the other thing is . . . you could come to my house. I already asked my mother."

"Really?" Veronica asked. "You mean I'm invited?"

Veronica and Hilary walked up the school steps together. Veronica was busy explaining her theory that Melody was actually a grown-up disguised as a kid—"a midget with lots of library cards, all with different names on them—"

"You know, Veronica . . . " Hilary interrupted. "I think Melody Hicks *is* her real name."

Veronica stared at Hilary. Hilary suddenly seemed so sure of herself.

"Look," said Hilary. "Who would invent a name like Melody Hicks?"

Veronica thought Hilary was probably right.

"I was just thinking the same thing," she said.

"Hi, Veronica," Amy called. Amy and Kimberly were standing at the top of the steps.

Veronica was surprised. *Now they want to be friends,* she thought. *Now that I already have a date for this afternoon.* Veronica ran up to them.

"Hi, Kimberly," she said. "Hi, Amy."

"How's your horse?" Amy asked her.

"What horse?" Veronica asked.

Amy and Kimberly ran in the door giggling.

Veronica stood there for a few seconds. Then she turned and looked around for Hilary. But Hilary had already gone in.

On Friday they always had French first thing in the morning. The French teacher was a tiny lady named Mademoiselle. She had a last name, too, but everyone just called her "Mademoiselle."

Mademoiselle had dark eyes that sparkled, and she danced around the classroom when she talked.

"Bonjour, classe," Mademoiselle sang out.

"Bonjour, Mademoiselle," mumbled the class.

"So," said Mademoiselle. "Are we ready with our lesson? Kimberly. In a nice loud voice, *s'il vous plaît.*"

27

Kimberly stood up. Everyone was supposed to recite a short paragraph. *"J'entre dans la salle de classe,"* Kimberly began. *"Je regarde autour de moi . . . "* Kimberly stopped.

Veronica waited for Kimberly to go on. Veronica was proud. She knew the whole paragraph by heart and she knew what every word meant. (*I enter the classroom. I look around me . . .*)

But Kimberly couldn't remember what came next. She stood there looking helplessly at Mademoiselle.

"Je vois les élèves," Veronica whispered. "I see the students."

"Je vois les élèves . . . " said Kimberly. She mumbled the rest and sat down.

Veronica couldn't wait for her turn.

"Veronica, *s'il vous plaît,"* said Mademoiselle.

Veronica stood up and marched up the aisle. Then she turned and walked to the door. Mademoiselle looked surprised.

"But, Veronica, where do you go?"

Veronica opened the door and went out. She stood outside the door and counted to ten. Then she flung open the door to the classroom and stepped in.

"J'entre dans la salle de classe," said Veronica in a nice loud voice.

Veronica looked slowly around, as if she were seeing the classroom for the first time. First she looked at the blackboard. Then she looked at the plants on the windowsill and the lights on the ceiling.

"Je regarde autour de moi." Veronica tried to make her mouth into funny shapes the way Mademoiselle did. It seemed to make French words come out better.

Veronica studied every face in the classroom. *"Je vois les élèves . . ."* Everyone stared back at her. Then Veronica swung around to face Mademoiselle. *" . . . et le professeur."* Veronica bowed to Mademoiselle. Mademoiselle smiled and bowed back. *"Je dis 'Bonjour' au professeur."*

Then Veronica marched back and sat down in her seat. *"Je prends ma place."* (*I take my seat,* she thought proudly.)

"Bravo!" shouted Mademoiselle. "Excellent, my dear, excellent!" Veronica beamed and looked around.

Kimberly and Amy had their heads bowed low over their desks. Their shoulders were shaking.

Everyone else in the class was either laughing or trying not to laugh. Everyone—except Hilary. Hilary smiled at Veronica.

During Social Studies, Veronica was quiet. She didn't raise her hand once.

There was a large map of the United States on the board. Everyone was supposed to choose a state and do a report on that state. The report was due in two weeks.

When Veronica's turn came to pick a state, she whispered, "Oh, I'll just take Rhode Island."

Rhode Island was very small. Veronica wanted everyone to see how modest she really was.

"She can't have Rhode Island!" Amy was furious. "I'm doing Rhode Island. My grandfather and grandmother live there."

"That's okay," said Veronica quickly. "I don't mind. I'll take another state."

"You can both do Rhode Island," the teacher said.

Amy glared at Veronica.

When Veronica changed for gym class, she hid behind a row of lockers. She always did that. She did not like to change in public like everyone else.

"Did you see her? Did you see Veronica the Show-off?" It was Amy's voice. "I couldn't believe her in French class."

"You mean Mademoiselle la Show-off?" Kimberly giggled.

Veronica suddenly felt very tired. She wanted to go home. Amy said "Veronica the Show-off" as if that were her real name. She was sure they always called her that.

I'll never say another word, Veronica promised herself. *I'll be quiet as a little mouse.*

"And how did you like the way she tried to steal Rhode Island from me?" said Amy.

"She just wants attention," said Kimberly. "She always wants attention."

Veronica waited behind the lockers until she heard everyone leave. She didn't want to go to gym. *No one will miss me anyway,* she thought.

Veronica buckled the belt of her blue gym tunic and peeked around the corner of a locker.

Hilary was standing there.

Hilary took Veronica's hand. "I thought you were wonderful in French class," she said.

"I don't want to go to gym," said Veronica in a small voice.

"Don't be silly," said Hilary. "Everyone has to go to gym."

"I want to go home," said Veronica.

"Don't be silly," said Hilary. "You're coming to my house this afternoon. Remember?"

Veronica let Hilary drag her by the hand to gym.

Strange Customs
❧ and Faraway Places

Hilary lived near the library, only five blocks away from Veronica.

When they got off the bus, it was snowing.

"Oh, boy," said Hilary. "And it's not even Thanksgiving yet." She stuck out her tongue and caught a snowflake. Veronica watched her.

"Speaking of snow," said Veronica, "you won't believe what happened to me when I was a little kid. It was just awful. You see, my father was pulling me around the block on this sled and, you see, I kept eating this snow. Straight off the ground. Dirty snow. Filthy snow. Snow that had been there for days. So anyway, I got sick. Very very sick. So sick they almost had to pump out my stomach." Then Veronica stuck out her tongue and caught a snowflake, too.

They came to Hilary's house.

"Here we are," said Hilary. Veronica looked up at the pink house with green shutters. It was four stories high and there were vines climbing all over it. Veronica carefully tucked her hair behind her ears. "My grandfather lives in a whole house, too," she said. "But it's much bigger."

"I like apartments better," said Hilary. "My cousin is so lucky. She lives in an apartment that is so small, the bed pops out of the wall."

"I live in an apartment," said Veronica.

A large silvery-gray dog met them at the door.

"Oh, you have a German shepherd," said Veronica.

"Wolf's not a shepherd," said Hilary.

"I love dogs," said Veronica. She petted Wolf. "Hi, Wolf," she said. Wolf sniffed her and looked up at her. He had a pointed face and very light-colored eyes. They were the lightest eyes Veronica had ever seen.

"He's a malamute, right?" asked Veronica. Veronica knew all about different breeds.

"Nope," said Hilary.

Veronica figured this dog was just a plain old mutt. She tried to think of something nice to say about him. Then she would tell Hilary all about her pure poodle, Lady Jane Grey.

"He looks just like a wolf," said Veronica.

"That's because he *is* one," said Hilary.

"A wolf?" Veronica jumped back. "A real wolf?"

"Mostly timber wolf," said Hilary. "He looks a little scary, but he's very gentle. And he never barks. Wolves don't bark, you know."

"Oh, I know," said Veronica, and she decided this was not the right time to talk about her poodle.

"Hilary, is that you? Are you home?" Someone was calling from upstairs.

Veronica looked up. A girl with bright red cheeks was running down the stairs. She had thick black braids and she was wearing a brown suede jacket with fringe on it.

Veronica thought she was beautiful. *She looks just like an Indian princess,* she thought. *Like Pocahontas!*

"This is my sister Samantha. She's fourteen," Hilary told Veronica.

Samantha was out of breath. "Hilary, listen," she said. "We've got to put the bed to sleep. Today. Right now."

"Right now?" Hilary asked.

"Well, it's already snowing," said Samantha.

Samantha smiled at Veronica. "Hi," she said. Veronica just stared at her.

"I guess you're right," said Hilary. "Oh, Veronica, do you mind?"

"Mind what?" asked Veronica. She wasn't sure she had heard right.

"Do you mind helping us put the bed to sleep?" asked Samantha.

"Sure I'll help," said Veronica.

"Oh, good for you!" shouted Samantha. And she hugged Veronica.

Veronica held very still with her arms stiff at her sides. She let herself be hugged. *She's hugging me!* she thought in amazement. *Me, Veronica!*

"But Veronica," Hilary whispered, "what about our investigation? What about you-know-who?"

"Oh, yeah, I forgot," said Veronica. She was still staring up at Samantha. "I guess Melody Hicks can wait, though," she said.

A lady with white hair came into the hallway. She kissed Hilary. "Hi, dear," she said.

"Mama," said Hilary, "this is Veronica."

Hilary's mother had a very young face even though her hair was white. "Well, Veronica," she said, "we're going to have to find you some clothes."

36

"Don't worry, Mama," said Samantha. "I'll find her something to wear."

Veronica followed Samantha and Hilary up a dark wooden staircase to the second floor. Veronica peeked in one room. There was a large brass bed with a patchwork quilt on it.

Veronica wondered if this was the bed they were putting to sleep. *It must be a game,* she thought. *Like playing house.*

Then Veronica saw Hilary's bed. It was simply a straw mat lying on the floor with a pad on top of it. The pad had a green-and-white slipcover on it. The bed was partly hidden by two Japanese screens.

Veronica was sure that putting a bed to sleep was a Japanese custom.

Veronica saw a pair of white pajamas with big sleeves hanging on the closet door.

"Are you wearing those for the ceremony?" she whispered to Hilary.

"What ceremony?" asked Hilary. "That's what I wear for karate."

Samantha took Veronica's hand. "Come to my room. I'll find you something to wear."

When Veronica saw Samantha's bed, she gasped.

Samantha's bed was a wooden platform that swung from chains attached to the ceiling. Veronica had never seen anything like it. A swinging bed!

"I guess your family really cares about beds," she said shyly to Samantha.

"What? Oh, I see what you mean. Yes, I guess we do," said Samantha. She handed Veronica a pair of striped work overalls, a red shirt, and a red-and-black checkered lumber jacket.

Veronica went into the bathroom and changed. When she came out, Samantha helped her roll up the sleeves of the lumber jacket.

"It's too big," said Samantha. "But you look so cute!"

Veronica smiled up at her. She felt very happy. No one had ever treated her this way.

"Here, let me put your hair up," said Samantha. And Veronica held still while Samantha put her hair into two little bunches. She had never worn her hair in bunches before.

"Don't you look sweet," said Samantha. "Well, come on then. Let's go!"

Veronica followed Samantha out of the room and down the stairs. She thought she would be willing to follow Samantha anywhere—anywhere in the whole world.

Hilary was waiting at the door. She was wearing work clothes, too.

They went outside and around the block. They stopped at a barber shop.

The barber came out and handed Samantha a plastic bag full of hair. "Nice fresh hair," he said, smiling at them. "I swept it up just for you."

"Oh, thank you," said Samantha. She handed the bag of hair to Hilary. "Hold it for now, then we can put it on the dolly."

They walked for another block until they came to a brick building.

"Wait out here a minute," said Samantha. "I'll run in and get the dolly from Peter."

A dolly? Veronica watched Samantha disappear into the building.

Samantha came out, pulling a big board with wheels on the bottom. "Here's the dolly," she called.

Farther down the block was a stable. Samantha went up to the man at the stable. "We're picking up the fresh manure we ordered," she told the man. "Could you please put it on the dolly?"

"Manure?" Veronica asked.

"To dump on the bed," said Hilary.

"But it will smell awful!" said Veronica. And she was sorry she hadn't had a chance to swing on the bed before they went and dumped manure on it.

"It conditions the soil over the winter," said Samantha. "You've got to put it on before the ground freezes over. Then we can plant vegetables again in the spring."

Veronica's eyes opened wide.

"ARE YOU TALKING ABOUT A GARDEN?" she shouted.

Both girls stared at her.

"Why, of course," said Samantha.

"What did you think?" asked Hilary.

And because they were the nicest girls Veronica had ever met, she told them what she had thought.

" . . . so anyway," said Veronica, "I figured it was this strange custom—like in this television special I saw about people in faraway lands." She stopped. "But what about the hair?" she asked.

"Full of nitrogen . . . good . . . good . . . fertil-izer." Samantha was laughing so hard she could hardly talk. Tears were running down Hilary's cheeks. Veronica was laughing, too. The three girls had to sit down on the dolly.

"Oh, that's wonderful!" Samantha said, and she gave Veronica another little hug.

Veronica felt lucky to have been so dumb.

The Little
Farmer 🐞

The garden was down the street from the stable. It was in a big lot.

"It's over an acre," said Samantha.

Veronica looked around. There were a lot of people working in the garden.

"That part's the community garden," said Hilary. "We all help there, but we also have our own little garden—our vegetable garden."

"There are still flowers," Veronica said.

"Oh, yes," said a lady Veronica didn't even know. "But, my dear, you should see it in the spring and summer." She sighed. "Daffodils, tulips—everything you can imagine."

"Sounds nice," said Veronica politely.

There was a tool shed in the corner of the lot. Hilary had a key to it. "We all share the tools," she said, and she opened the tool shed.

"Oh, please, please can I use the pitchfork?" Veronica asked.

"Of course," said Samantha.

A big lady helped them dump the manure in a pile on the vegetable bed. Then they began to spread it around.

The pitchfork was heavy. Veronica worked hard. She worked harder than she ever had in her whole life. Her arms began to hurt. She was dirty and smelly, but she felt good.

"This is fun!" she kept saying when everyone told her to take a rest.

When they finished, they returned the tools to the shed.

"So that's putting a bed to sleep," said Veronica as they walked back to Hilary's house.

Hilary's mother was waiting on the stoop. She seemed worried.

"Veronica," she said, "shouldn't you telephone your mother?"

"Oh, it's okay," said Veronica. "I usually go to the library after school anyway. Just as long as I'm home before dark."

"But it *is* dark," said Hilary's mother.

Veronica looked around. It was dark. She hadn't even noticed.

"Yipes!" said Veronica.

Hilary's mother took her into the kitchen.

"But I'm so dirty," said Veronica.

"Don't worry about that," said Hilary's mother. "Just call your mother. The phone's over there."

Veronica called her mother.

"Where are you, sweetheart?" Her mother sounded worried.

"Oh, Mom, I'm at Hilary's. You won't believe what we just did. We—"

"Sweetheart," her mother said, "you can tell me all about it some other time. The baby-sitter is already here and I'm on my way out."

"But Mom—" said Veronica.

"Hurry, dear," her mother said, and hung up.

"Is everything all right?" Hilary's mother was watching her.

"My mother *was* worried," said Veronica. "She was worried sick about me. I've got to go right home. She just can't wait to hear all about what we did."

"Thank you for helping," Hilary's mother said. "Why don't you just wear those clothes home."

"Oh, *thank* you," said Veronica. "Thank you, *everybody!*" she called.

It had stopped snowing, but it was very cold.

The cold air felt wonderful. Veronica started skipping. Veronica hardly ever skipped.

"I am a happy farmer . . . " she sang. People coming home from work looked at her and smiled.

I'll bet I smell awful, Veronica thought happily.

When she passed the library, she skipped right into Miss Markham.

"Oh, Miss Markham, Miss Markham!" she shouted. "You'll never guess what I did!"

"Why, Veronica, don't you look healthy." Miss Markham looked surprised, but she seemed happy to see Veronica.

"I put a bed to bed. I mean I put vegetables to sleep . . . " Suddenly Veronica remembered the way she had acted at the library. She looked down at the sidewalk.

"You mean the community garden on 89th Street?" Miss Markham asked. Veronica nodded.

"I have a plot there, too," said Miss Markham.

"Um, Miss Markham . . . I meant to tell you . . . um . . . I'm sorry . . . " Veronica began.

"Yes, Veronica, I know. I'm sorry, too. I don't usually let a whole series go out of the library. But you see, Melody's mother came in—"

"Melody's *mother?*" Veronica asked.

"Yes, you see, Melody's stuck in bed with the chicken pox—"

"Melody Hicks has the chicken pox?" Veronica couldn't believe it. "Oh, Miss Markham, does she have it bad? As bad as me? I had the worst case of the chicken pox the doctor ever saw. I almost had to go to the hospital. Is she simply covered with spots? Is she itching like crazy?"

Miss Markham laughed. "I don't know, Veronica."

"I'll bet she doesn't have it as bad as I did," Veronica said.

Miss Markham looked at her watch. Veronica tried to think of something to say; she didn't want Miss Markham to leave.

"Oh, Miss Markham, I was wondering . . . you see, I have to do this report on Rhode Island. Do you think there would be any books in the library on Rhode Island? I know it's a very small state."

"I'm sure we have something." Miss Markham smiled. "We have books on everything." She turned to go. "Come see me soon," she called.

Veronica skipped the rest of the way home.

The Friends
of Polly Winkler

Early Saturday morning the telephone rang. Veronica ran to get it.

"Hi, Daddy!" she shouted. "I knew you would call!"

"Um," said a little voice, "Veronica?"

"Huh?" said Veronica.

"It's me, Hilary," said the little voice. "Veronica, listen. We don't have a minute to lose. In fact, it may already be too late!"

Veronica was confused. Hilary went on. "I looked it up in my dictionary. It's much more serious than I thought."

"Looked up *what* in your dictionary?" Veronica asked her.

"Smuggler. Smuggler," Hilary whispered. "They don't just steal things, Veronica. They sneak them out of the country. And I suspect that Melody is on her way to China right this minute."

"China?" Veronica gasped.

"Well, maybe South America. I think South America is more likely," said Hilary. "Just think. Right this very minute Melody Hicks is flying down to Brazil with a suitcase full of Polly Winklers."

"What?" Veronica was horrified.

"Oh, they may not even *be* in her suitcase," said Hilary. "She might have put them on microfilm. Did you know that you can fit every single Polly Winkler on one tiny piece of microfilm?"

"I already know that," said Veronica. "I saw a spy movie about that."

"Veronica," said Hilary, "I've been doing a lot of thinking and I'm pretty sure I know where that microfilm is."

"Where?" asked Veronica.

"In her *undershirt!*" said Hilary.

"Why, that sneaky little rat!" Veronica was furious. "And I thought she was in bed with the chicken pox!"

"Huh?" Now Hilary was confused.

"That's what Miss Markham said." Veronica told Hilary how she had bumped into Miss Markham the evening before.

"Well, then she probably does have the chicken pox." Hilary sounded disappointed. She sighed. "So Melody Hicks isn't a dangerous smuggler."

"I guess not," Veronica admitted. "She's just a kid with the chicken pox."

No one said anything for a while. Veronica began to feel worried. Now that there was no "mysterious disappearance," what would they talk about?

Then Hilary giggled. "So old Melody has the chicken pox."

"Yup," said Veronica. "Good old Melody has the chicken pox."

"Well, maybe we should send her a card," said Hilary. "You know, to cheer her up."

"That would be awfully nice of us," said Veronica. "Let's do it!"

They met in front of Sherman's Stationery Store. Veronica felt rich. Her mother had given her enough money for two ice cream sodas—one for her and one for Hilary.

"But we have to buy the card out of this money. I didn't want to tell my mom about Melody,"

Veronica told Hilary. "Even so, we'll have enough left over for ice cream cones."

They stood outside Sherman's, looking in through the window.

"The man in there is so mean," said Hilary.

"I know," said Veronica. "He hates kids." She took Hilary's hand. "Well, let's go in," she said. But neither of them moved.

"Um . . . Veronica. I was just wondering. What kind of ice cream sodas would they have been?" Hilary asked.

"Oh, I don't know," Veronica said. "Delicious ones. Maybe chocolate chocolate-chip with two scoops of ice cream, loaded with whipped cream. One or maybe even two cherries on top."

"Oh, my," said Hilary. "Just think of us giving up all that for Melody."

"I know," said Veronica. "I just hope she appreciates all this suffering."

Veronica suddenly felt very brave. She pulled Hilary into the stationery store.

They were only a few steps inside when a man's voice boomed out, "Well, girls, what do you want?"

Veronica spoke in her most grown-up voice.

"We happen to be looking for a card. We happen to have plenty of money to pay for it, and we happen to want the very best."

"Well, what kind of card do you want?" the man asked crossly. He pointed to the rows and rows of cards. "Birthday, anniversary, Christmas, sympathy—"

"Sympathy," said Veronica. "That's exactly what we want—a sympathy card."

Hilary poked Veronica in the side. "We don't want sympathy!" she whispered.

"Of course we do," Veronica whispered.

The man didn't look so cross anymore. "Sympathy cards are over there," he said.

Hilary followed Veronica. She kept poking Veronica in the back. "But Veronica, don't you know what 'sympathy' means?"

"Of course I do," said Veronica. "I know *exactly* what sympathy means. It means we *sympathize* with Melody. It means we know just how she feels. And, boy do I know how it feels to have the chicken pox, except of course I had it much worse—much more worse."

"But . . ." said Hilary.

Veronica didn't pay any more attention to Hilary. She marched over to the rows of sympathy cards. Then she pulled out a card, opened it, and read it carefully. She closed the card and placed it back on the rack. She picked out another card and read that one, too. Hilary was watching her. Veronica closed the card.

Veronica didn't want to admit it, but she didn't understand the messages on the cards. There were some very big words. "Melody would never understand them," she muttered to herself.

"Well, girls?"

Veronica and Hilary turned around. The man was watching them. "Find anything?" he asked suspiciously.

"A few things," said Veronica in her grown-up voice. "But don't you have anything more . . . well . . . more *humorous?*"

For a moment Hilary looked as if she were going to faint. She blinked her eyes very fast. Then she pulled herself up straight and looked the man right in the eye.

"Mister," she said. "My friend does not mean humorous in a funny way. She means more . . . um . . . cheerful."

The man stared at Hilary. Then he growled,

"Just what you see in front of your eyes," and he went back to the counter.

"Veronica," whispered Hilary, "I have something to tell you. You send sympathy cards when someone is dead."

Veronica stared at Hilary. She didn't believe her.

"I should know," Hilary went on. "When my grandmother died, my mother got tons of them. And they never say 'dead' or 'died' or anything like that."

Veronica's face turned red. "Now what are we going to do?" she asked. "We'll have to buy one anyway or he'll throw us out."

Quickly Veronica found a card that said BEYOND LIFE'S DOORWAY on the front. She took it to the counter and paid for it.

"Now we need a card for someone who is sick," she told the man.

"I'm sorry to hear that," said the man in a gentle voice. "Troubles always seem to come at the same time."

"I know," said Veronica.

It wasn't easy to find just the right get-well card

for Melody. There were two kinds of cards: one kind had birds and flowers and sweet messages; then there were the funny cards.

"Kids like funny cards," said Veronica. She showed Hilary the one she thought was the funniest.

It had a cartoon of a very ugly lady on the front. CHEER UP, it said. YOU'LL SOON BE YOUR OLD SELF AGAIN. And when you opened it up, it said, TOO BAD!

"Isn't that a little mean?" asked Hilary.

"Don't worry," said Veronica. "It's the thought that counts."

"But the thought—" said Hilary.

"Look, Hilary." Veronica was feeling very sure of herself again. "Those stupid cards with birds and flowers are for grown-ups. The funny cards are for kids. Now it wouldn't exactly be in good taste to get a kid a card that was meant for a grown-up, would it?"

"I guess you're right," said Hilary.

When they got outside, Veronica said proudly, "Now we don't even have enough money left over for ice cream cones. I never heard of anything so nice in my whole life."

"I know what you mean," said Hilary. "You

know, Veronica, doing good deeds like this makes me feel *taller* somehow."

They stopped in a drug store and borrowed a telephone book. They looked up "Hicks," hoping to find Melody's address.

"There are hundreds of Hicks," Veronica wailed. "We'll never know which one she is."

"Let's ask Miss Markham," said Hilary.

"Good idea," said Veronica.

When they got into the children's room, a little boy ran up to Veronica.

"She's back!" he yelled. "That girl is back." Veronica stared down at him.

"It's me, Jeremy," said the little boy. "Did the police catch her yet? Did they catch that girl who tore your book into a million pieces and stuffed it down the garbage pail?"

Miss Markham smiled when Hilary and Veronica told her about the card for Melody.

"How nice," she said. "I'll make sure it gets to her."

"We have to sign it," said Hilary.

Veronica and Hilary found a table and sat down. Jeremy sat down, too, and watched them.

"I think we should just write, 'From the Friends

of Polly Winkler Fan Club,' " said Veronica.

". . . in care of the Harding Branch of the library," said Hilary.

"Yes," said Veronica. "Then she can thank us."

Veronica wrote very neatly. When she finished, she turned the card over and wrote something on the back.

"What are you writing now?" Hilary asked.

"Oh, just a little P.S." said Veronica.

"P.S. what?" asked Hilary.

Veronica showed Hilary:

" P.S. By the way if you are finally finished reading The Clue in the Whispering Willow, could you please get it back. Some people haven't even gotten to read it yet."

"Oh, Veronica," said Hilary when she had finished reading the P.S. "That doesn't sound too nice."

"Oh, yes it does," said Veronica. "Listen." And she read it out loud in her sweetest voice. "You see?" she asked Hilary.

"It does sound better when you read it," Hilary admitted.

"It sounds beautiful!" said Jeremy.

56

&ranch; Library Blues

Veronica and Hilary stopped by the library every afternoon to see if anything had come from Melody.

By Wednesday Veronica was disgusted. "I told you she was like that. No manners at all. And after all we did for her."

"Oh, come on, Veronica," said Hilary. "We didn't do *that* much. We just sent her a card."

"And what about the ice cream sodas we could have had and what about giving up our whole Saturday afternoon just to be kind to her and what about . . ." Veronica went on and on.

"Please stop," Hilary finally said. "You're giving me a headache."

On Thursday Hilary had karate class. Veronica decided to go to the library and see if there were any books about Rhode Island for her Social Studies report. It was raining hard.

As soon as she got into the children's room, she

went to the Polly Winkler shelf just to see if Melody had returned any books.

Veronica blinked. All the Polly Winklers were back on the shelf. She looked more closely. They were all back except one—*The Clue in the Whispering Willow*.

"On purpose!" Veronica shouted. "Just to be mean to me!"

She ran to get Miss Markham. Miss Markham was standing on a low stool with a big pile of books in her arms.

"Oh, Miss Markham. Guess what. She did it on purpose." Veronica danced around Miss Markham. "We've got proof!"

"Just a minute, Veronica," Miss Markham said. "I'll be right with you."

"But Miss Markham, you've got to see . . ." Veronica pulled on Miss Markham's arm.

Miss Markham dropped all the books on the floor. "Oh, honestly, Veronica," she said.

Then Miss Markham did the strangest thing. She sank down onto the stool and covered her face with her hands.

Veronica stared at Miss Markham. "What's the matter?" she asked. Then she looked around. For the first time Veronica noticed that the library was much noisier than usual. And there were buckets all over the place. Veronica looked up. Water was dripping from the ceiling. Some little kids were sailing paper boats in the buckets. Jeremy was jumping up and down in a little puddle on the floor. He was singing:

"Went to the doctor and the doctor said, 'No more *monkeys* jumping on the bed.' Went to the doctor . . ."

"What's going on?" Veronica asked.

Miss Markham raised her head. "A pipe broke," she said. "This place is falling apart."

"Can't they fix it?" Veronica asked.

"Oh, yes, I guess they'll fix it. But that's just the beginning. The library has had its budget cut. We don't have any money. The Story Lady won't be coming anymore."

"But they can't do that!" said Veronica.

Miss Markham sighed. "And they've cut our hours. Starting today, the library will be closing early."

"They can't *do* that!" Veronica was very angry. "I have to do Rhode Island."

Veronica helped Miss Markham pick up the

books. Then Miss Markham helped Veronica find books on Rhode Island.

Veronica sat down at a table and opened a book called *All About the States*. She tried to read the chapter on Rhode Island, but the library was too noisy. Veronica closed the book and thought about Melody. She decided she would not say anything more to Miss Markham.

This is a private war, she thought. *Between me and Melody.*

She watched Miss Markham, who was trying to get the little kids to sit down and find themselves something to read. But Miss Markham had so many other things to do.

"Hey, Miss Markham," said Veronica. "Maybe I could help. I'm awfully good with little kids."

"That would be just great!" said Miss Markham.

Veronica went over to the children, who were splashing in the buckets.

"All right, boys and girls," she yelled. "Now I am going to find you some nice books to keep you quiet."

"Come back later," said a little boy with red hair and glasses.

"No more *monkeys* jumping on the bed . . ." Jeremy sang.

60

Veronica put her finger to her lips. Librarians always did that. She waited for silence, but no one seemed to notice.

Then Veronica got an idea. She went to her notebook and tore out a piece of paper. She ripped it into little pieces and wrote a big number on each one—from one to ten.

She handed each child a number.

"What's this?" asked Jeremy.

"That's your number," said Veronica. "You have to sit down and wait for your number to be called. Then I will find you your own personal book."

"My mother gets numbers like this at the bakery," said a pale little girl with stringy blond hair.

Before long, all the children were sitting quietly, waiting for their numbers to be called.

The pale little girl had number one. Veronica took her hand and led her to the picture-book shelf. "Here is a book you will love," said Veronica. It was called *The Lion Who Wouldn't Stand Still.* It had been Veronica's favorite book when she was small.

"I don't like books about lions," said the little girl.

"All children like books about lions," said Veronica.

"Well, I don't," said the little girl. "I like *real* books. Books about lions aren't real."

"Oh," said Veronica. She found the little girl a book about a visit from Grandmother. She held it out to her.

The little girl leaned forward and studied the cover.

"No!" she said. "*Real* books—like *Peter Rabbit*."

"Rabbits are real?" Veronica asked.

"Yes," said the little girl. "So are bears."

"I see," said Veronica. And she found the little girl a book called *Rabbit Family Goes to Town*.

The little girl was very happy.

"Creatures and monsters, please," said the little boy with red hair and glasses. It was his turn.

"Creatures and monsters coming up," said Veronica cheerfully.

"I'm going to marry Veronica," Veronica heard Jeremy whisper to Ruthie. Veronica blushed and pretended not to hear.

"Number eight," Veronica called. "Who has number eight?"

"What's this say?" Ruthie showed Veronica her slip of paper.

"That's an eight," said Veronica. "Well, what kind of book can I get for you?"

"I don't want a book," said Ruthie.

"You don't want a book?" asked Veronica.

"No, thank you," said Ruthie shyly. "I just want a number." And she sat there quietly, staring at her number.

"Don't turn pages like that!" Veronica said to Jeremy when she saw him scrunching up pages. "You'll ruin the book. In the library we *respect* books. Pages are turned like *this*." And she showed him.

Soon the children's room was quiet. Veronica was about to go back to work on her report when she saw Chris standing next to Miss Markham's desk.

Chris lived across the hall from Veronica. Chris was with his best friend Peter. Both boys had been in Veronica's class when she went to public school.

Veronica suddenly realized she was sitting with a bunch of little kids. She was embarrassed. She jumped up and went over to Chris and Peter.

"Hi," she said. "What are you doing here?"

"We're waiting to ask Miss Markham something, if you don't mind," said Peter. He did not look pleased to see Veronica.

"Well, it just so happens that Miss Markham is very busy, and it just so happens that I am helping Miss Markham, so you have to ask me," said Veronica.

"We would rather talk to a grown-up," said Peter.

Veronica was curious. She went to the card file and pretended to look something up. Then she heard Chris whisper to Peter, "I'm sure it's under G for *Goblin*."

"No!" Peter whispered back. "It's *Best—B* for *Best—Best Goblin Jokes from Around the World*."

"Goblin jokes!" Veronica shouted. "Now, aren't you a little too old for that? That's a first-grade book!"

Peter and Chris looked down at the floor.

"My, my," said Veronica. "I am surprised at you." She took each boy by the arm. "Now let me recommend something more for your . . . um . . . age group. An orange biography, perhaps . . ."

Chris and Peter pulled away from Veronica and started running down the stairs.

"Boy, that Veronica!" she heard Peter say. "What a show-off! She never changes."

"I do *too* change," Veronica called down the

stairs. "I have *too* changed. I've changed so much you wouldn't even recognize me."

"Ha!" Peter called up the stairs.

Veronica was sure she had changed. She felt like a different person. She couldn't understand why no one seemed to notice. *It must be way down deep*, she thought. *Way, way down deep!*

Job Wanted

"I can't stand it!" Amy was standing next to Veronica's desk. "Veronica got a better mark. And after all the work I did!"

The Social Studies teacher was handing back the reports on the states. Veronica covered up the red writing at the top of her report, but it was too late. Amy had already seen it.

"Excellent!" the teacher had written. "Interesting facts! Good research!"

"Who does she think she is? Miss America?" Amy was so angry she forgot to lower her voice. "Besides," she said to Kimberly, "someone told me Veronica used the library."

"Don't be silly," the teacher snapped. "Everyone is supposed to use the library."

Amy was quiet for the rest of the class period, but she spent the whole lunch hour telling Kimberly (and anyone else who would listen) that Veronica was a show-off *and* a cheat.

Almost every day Veronica and Hilary went to the library and helped Miss Markham. They found books for the little kids to read. They straightened out the bookshelves. Then they usually went to Hilary's house and took Wolf out for a walk.

Hilary's mother invited Veronica for dinner a few times. After dinner Samantha always walked Veronica home. Veronica was allowed to go home by herself, but she liked to be walked home by Samantha. Samantha would hold her hand and ask her questions about school. Veronica never talked. She just nodded her head "yes" or shook it for "no." She still felt shy with Samantha.

Christmas was coming and Veronica was sure she was going to spend the vacation with her father in California.

"I'm going to fly to the coast," she told Hilary. "I'm going to lie on a beach and bash in the sun."

"*Bash* in the sun?" asked Hilary.

"That's what they call it out there," said Veronica.

"Oh, Veronica, don't you mean *bask*? Bask in the sun?" asked Hilary.

"I'm going to do that, too," said Veronica happily.

Two days before the Christmas holiday, *The Clue in the Whispering Willow* finally came back to the library.

"Just think!" said Veronica. "Melody paid an absolute *fortune* in overdue fines—and just to be mean to me!"

Veronica and Hilary took the book to the science room at their school and looked at it under a microscope. Veronica claimed she saw "millions of Melody's chicken pox germs crawling all over the place."

"All I see is my eyelash," said Hilary.

Veronica took the book home. She placed it carefully on the night table next to her bed, but she didn't open it. She had too much to do. She wanted to pack her suitcase so that she would be ready when her father called.

Then she noticed a postcard propped up against the lamp on her night table. She picked it up.

On the front of the postcard was a picture of a beach. But it wasn't a beach in California. There were palm trees on the beach and the people in the picture were wearing grass skirts and necklaces made out of flowers.

Veronica turned over the card and read:

How's my big girl? You would love Hawaii. Lots of sun. Good swimming and sailing. See you next year!

Dad

Veronica tore the postcard into tiny pieces. That made her feel even worse, so she spent the rest of the afternoon taping it back together.

On the day before vacation Veronica felt miserable, but she didn't say anything to Hilary. She didn't want Hilary to know she wasn't going to California.

Hilary had to return some Polly Winklers, so they walked to the library after school.

Veronica was having trouble paying attention to what Hilary was saying. She was wondering if, by any chance, her father was going to surprise her with a plane ticket to Hawaii.

"Veronica!" said Hilary. "Did you hear what I said?"

Veronica nodded.

"Well, do you want to or not?" asked Hilary.

"Want to what?" asked Veronica.

"Do you want to help me pack my suitcase?"

"For what?" asked Veronica.

"Veronica, I told you! I'm going to my cousin Timmy's for the vacation."

Veronica stopped walking. She stared at Hilary. "What? You did not tell me any such thing. Oh, Hilary, you *can't* go away."

"I did *too* tell you. I told you weeks ago. You just didn't listen," Hilary said. "Oh, Veronica, I'm so excited. It's so much fun there. They have this big house in the country and I have all these boy cousins—"

"Well, you don't have to keep talking about it," Veronica said crossly.

Hilary looked surprised, but she didn't say anything more about her trip.

When they got to the library, Veronica said, "I'll just wait downstairs. I don't really feel like going up." Veronica had a big lump in her throat. She was afraid she was going to cry. How could Hilary do this to her?

She tried to read the notices on the library bulletin board, but they were all blurry. There was a sign that said the library would be open over the Christmas vacation. Veronica tried to read another sign through her tears. It was a notice about a missing dog—a white-and-black one. That made Veronica so sad she quickly found another sign to read:

```
JOB WANTED — CAN DO ANYTHING

Walk Your Dog — I am a dog exspert
Tuter Your Child — Six or seven yr old
              perferred.
Water Your Plants — I will talk to them
      for no adisionel charge.

      FOR INFORMATION CALL
  MELODY HICKS, AGE 10    877-3034
```

Veronica dried her eyes quickly and read the sign again.

Then she copied Melody's phone number on her assignment pad. *So I can let her know what I think of her.* Veronica was horrified. *What a show-off! Kids like that have to be punished!*

Veronica dug into her book bag and took out a red marker. She corrected all the spelling on Melody's sign by circling each word in red. Since she wasn't always sure of the right way to spell some of the words, she just wrote "SP!!!" above each one. Then she thought for a few seconds. Carefully, she gave the job notice a "C-minus" just like a teacher. "Nice try," she wrote across the top in big red letters. That was the most insulting thing she could think of saying.

"What are you doing?" Hilary was standing behind her staring at the sign.

"Oh, Hilary, can you believe it? Have you ever seen such a show-off?" Veronica was very excited.

"You are supposed to show off when you are looking for a job," said Hilary.

"And look what I wrote! Isn't it funny? Boy, did I fix her!" Veronica was proud.

"Veronica," said Hilary. "You shouldn't have done that."

Veronica Gives
❧ Some Advice

"Don't you have a nicer suitcase?" Veronica asked.

Hilary was putting her clothes into a worn-out brown leather bag.

"You really ought to take a more attractive suitcase," Veronica told her. "Now, I have a complete set of matching luggage. You really ought to get some *luggage*."

Hilary didn't say anything. She hadn't said a word since they left the library.

"Don't you see?" said Veronica. "I only did it for Melody's own good. She would have never gotten a job with a sign like that."

Hilary left the room. She came back holding a red toothbrush.

"Well, I don't see why you always have to be on Melody's side," said Veronica.

Veronica watched Hilary wrap some toilet paper around the toothbrush.

"Oh, no, Hilary! Don't you have an overnight case? You really ought to get one. I've got the cutest pink one with a million compartments—for soap, toothbrushes, perfume, combs . . . but, of course, I do an awful lot of traveling."

Hilary was piling socks next to her suitcase. Heavy woolen socks and little pink socks with lace around the cuffs.

"Eek! No, Hilary! You can't take those socks. Don't you have any regular socks? Listen, Hilary, let me give you some advice. No one in the world wears socks like that. They'll laugh their heads off when they see those socks. You might as well know the *truth*."

Hilary went to her closet and took out a pair of jeans.

Veronica began wandering around Hilary's room. She looked at a Beginner Swimming Card that was taped to Hilary's mirror.

"I can't believe you learned to swim in a city pool," said Veronica. "You poor kid. We go to Maine every summer and swim in my grandfather's private lake."

There was a color photo of Hilary's family next to the card. Hilary and Samantha were very young. Samantha was crying, Hilary was blinking her eyes, and their mother was laughing. Veronica looked at it closely.

"How come your mother doesn't dye her hair or something? You know, she really should. She looks terribly old with white hair. My mother says that every woman has a duty to look young and my mother looks so young, no one can believe she has *me!*"

Veronica looked over at Hilary. Hilary was sitting on the floor folding a pair of green mittens. She seemed to be daydreaming. She kept folding the thumbs of the mittens and unfolding them again.

"She should really dye her hair," said Veronica.

Hilary looked up at the ceiling. Her eyes began to flutter.

"Look, Hilary," said Veronica. "You've got to stop blinking like that. You should see what it looks like. It looks absolutely *weird!*"

Veronica was glad she had finally said that. Hilary's blink had bothered her for months. *I'm only trying to help her,* Veronica told herself.

Veronica couldn't think of any more helpful advice, so she plopped herself down on a cushion.

Hilary's dog, Wolf, was trying to take a nap on the same cushion. He jumped up and stared at Veronica.

"Make your dog stop looking at me like that." Veronica giggled nervously. "He looks so vicious!"

Hilary was still folding the same pair of mittens.

Veronica suddenly had a strange feeling. It was as if Hilary were slipping away. It was as if Hilary had already gone away, even though she was sitting right there. It was scary.

"Remember the garden?" Veronica asked in a loud, cheerful voice. "Remember how we put the bed to sleep? I can't wait to help you plant vegetables. I can't wait for spring."

Veronica wished it were already spring. She wished it were any time but right now. Right now something horrible was happening.

Hilary didn't even look up. Veronica had to try something else.

"Look, Hilary, you may be right about the sign." (It was a hard thing to admit.) "But, you see, the reason I know so much about Melody Hicks is . . . well . . . you see, I used to be a show-off myself."

Hilary looked straight at Veronica. "Used to be?" she asked.

Why was Hilary staring at her like that? "You don't think I still *am,* do you?"

"Oh, Veronica." Hilary sighed and stood up. She stuffed the green mittens into her suitcase. "I don't mind that part so much. It's the part where you make me feel bad."

Suddenly Veronica was in a big hurry to leave. She found her jacket and put it on.

"I don't know what you mean," Veronica mumbled as she buttoned her jacket.

"You know," said Hilary. "The part where you hurt my feelings. Hey, Veronica! Veronica! Where are you going?"

But Veronica was already gone.

"Aren't you hungry?" the baby-sitter asked her.

Veronica shook her head. She couldn't even eat her lamb chop, and lamb chops were her favorite food.

She went to her room and closed the door. She looked around for something to do, so she wouldn't have to think anymore.

The Clue in the Whispering Willow was lying on the table next to her bed. Veronica picked it up and lay down on her bed. She read the first page over and over. She didn't seem to be able to understand what the words meant. She thought about Melody and about how much easier it was to have an enemy than a friend.

Veronica shook her head very hard. She didn't want to think about friends. *All they do is go away and leave you anyway,* she told herself. *Everybody does that.*

Veronica decided to go to sleep. She turned off the light and crawled under the covers. She was still wearing her clothes.

Then she lay there trying to make herself go right to sleep.

The television was on very loud. The baby-sitter was watching her favorite rerun. Jo-Ann only liked programs she had seen before.

The laugh track was especially loud. Every time Veronica heard those fake laughs, she shivered. She buried her head under the pillow and began to cry. Once she started crying, she couldn't stop.

When a telephone rang, Veronica thought it was part of the TV program until she heard the baby-sitter knocking on her door.

"It's for you, Veronica!" Jo-Ann shouted. "And hurry up. You're going to make me miss the end of my show."

Veronica crawled out from under the covers.

She went to the phone on the hall table. She picked up the receiver and listened. She heard crackling. It sounded like a long-distance call.

"Hello?" she said.

"Hi, it's Samantha. Listen, Veronica. Hilary wants to talk to you."

"Where are you?" Veronica asked.

"At the airport," said Samantha.

"You're calling all the way from the airport?" Veronica shouted.

"Hold on," said Samantha. Then Veronica heard Hilary's voice.

"I just wanted to say good-bye," said Hilary. "And I wanted to tell you to have fun in California."

"Thank you," Veronica said politely. "But I'm not exactly going to California."

"You're not?" asked Hilary. "What happened?"

"Oh, it doesn't matter," said Veronica. "I didn't really want to go anyway. But, listen, Hilary. I was thinking . . . you could borrow my pink overnight case—you know, the one with all the compartments? I guess I won't be needing it."

"Thank you," said Hilary. Then she giggled. "It's a little late for that. My plane leaves in ten minutes."

"Oh, yeah, I guess it is," said Veronica.

"Guess what," said Hilary.

"What?" asked Veronica.

"I'm going to miss you," said Hilary.

"Me, too!" said Veronica. "I mean, I'm going to miss you, too."

"Well, I've got to go. Bye," said Hilary.

Veronica went back to her room. She looked in the mirror. Her eyes were swollen, her face was streaked with dirt and dried-up tears, her clothes were all wrinkled, but she had a big grin on her face.

Veronica flopped down on her bed. "She likes me anyway!" she said over and over until she fell asleep.

Saturday
ॐ at Home

When Veronica woke up the next morning, she felt strange. For a moment she didn't know where she was. She was no longer on top of the covers. She was under them. Her bed was very neat. The sheets felt fresh and clean.

Her wrists tickled. Veronica pulled her arms out from under the covers. She was wearing a white flannel nightgown with red ribbon and lace around the cuffs. It was very pretty, but it wasn't her nightgown.

"Hey!" Veronica shouted. "How did this get on me?"

She jumped out of bed and ran into the living room. Her mother was sitting at her desk.

"Hey!" said Veronica. "I'm wearing someone else's nightgown."

Her mother didn't look up. She said, "It's an early Christmas present. Your other nightgown was a disgrace."

Veronica hugged herself in her soft new night-gown. "I love it," she said. "But I don't even remember you putting it on me."

"You were asleep," her mother said. "Believe me, that is the last time I'll ever ask that Jo-Ann to baby-sit. I came home exhausted and there she was in front of the TV getting Munchy Crunchies all over my good chair."

"What about me?" Veronica asked shyly.

"You were a sight! I found you fast asleep with your clothes on. Your face was absolutely caked with dirt. Now, Veronica, how many times must I tell you how important it is to take care of your complexion? If you don't start now, you will be sorry later."

Veronica's mother finally looked up. She smiled when she saw Veronica in the new nightgown. "Well, that's better. That's the way my little girl should look."

Veronica twirled around. Then she ran to the living room window. It was snowing hard.

"Wow!" said Veronica. "A blizzard! Boy, am I glad I didn't go to California."

"Oh, darling, are you disappointed?" her mother asked.

But Veronica didn't answer. The snow looked

so beautiful swirling around like that. There was so much wind, the window was rattling.

Veronica wanted to wear her nightgown all day. She curled up in a chair in the living room with her Polly Winkler Mystery Story. Her mother was busy writing late Christmas cards.

Veronica kept looking up from her book to watch the snow. The snow was sticking to every-thing. The branches of the trees were covered with snow.

"It looks like fairyland," said Veronica.

Her mother stopped writing. She stood up and went to the window. For a long time she just stood there looking out at the snow.

"It does look like fairyland," Veronica's mother said after a while.

Veronica was pleased that her mother knew about fairyland.

Veronica was reading very slowly. *Maybe I've gotten too old for Polly Winklers,* she thought.

The only interesting part was when Polly and her little brother Scotty found a message hidden in the trunk of an old willow tree:

"It seems to be written in invisible ink," declared Polly, her blue eyes sparkling with excitement.

83

Veronica read that line over and over. She was puzzled. How did Polly know it was written in invisible ink? It was just a blank piece of paper.

Veronica closed the book and stared out the window some more.

She found herself wondering when *The Clue in the Whispering Willow* was due back.

Veronica pulled the card out of the pocket. The book was due back the first week in January. She had plenty of time to finish it.

Veronica slipped the card back into the pocket, but it wouldn't go all the way in. She tried to push it down, but the card just wouldn't go in straight.

There was something stuck in the bottom of the pocket.

Veronica tried to stick her finger into the pocket, but she was afraid of ripping it.

She tried to peek in the pocket.

"Mom," she said, "could I borrow your letter opener?"

"As long as you put it back where you found it," her mother said.

Veronica got the letter opener and carefully slid it into the pocket. She moved it around. A piece of paper slipped out. It was all folded up.

Veronica unfolded it carefully. It was a small piece of stationery. There was printing at the top: FROM THE DESK OF MELODY HICKS.

Why had Melody stuck a piece of blank stationery into the pocket of the book? What did it mean? All at once Veronica thought she knew.

"It seems to be written in invisible ink," Veronica declared.

"What did you say?" her mother asked. She stared at Veronica.

"Nothing," said Veronica. She was very excited.

"Good book?" her mother asked.

"Very good," said Veronica. She quickly tucked the piece of paper back into the pocket of the book. Then she turned back to find out how Polly Winkler read messages written in invisible ink.

"Lemon juice! It must be written in lemon juice!" exclaimed Polly. "All we have to do is to hold it near a source of heat—a candle, or even a light bulb. That will make the invisible ink turn brown. Then we will be able to read the mysterious message."

"Wow!" said her little brother Scotty, looking up at his sister with an admiring gaze.

Veronica looked around the living room. There were three lamps, but the one next to her chair had a three-way bulb. *I'll use that one*, she decided. *It is probably the hottest.*

But now she had to wait for her mother to leave the room.

Veronica wondered if Melody needed a partner in the dog-walking business. She hoped Melody wouldn't mind that Veronica was younger than she was. *I act old for my age*, Veronica told herself. *Maybe we can start a detective club and go around solving mysteries together. We could start with easy ones, like a missing dog or something, and work our way up to regular crimes—bank robberies and things like that!*

Veronica was so thrilled with that idea, she wanted to call Melody right away and make a date with her. But she figured she'd better read the message first.

When Veronica's mother finally left the room to make some lunch, Veronica stood up on the chair and took the lamp shade off the lamp. Then she turned the light all the way up. It was very bright. Veronica blinked.

She held the piece of paper near the light bulb for a few seconds. Nothing happened. Veronica put the paper even closer to the light bulb. She waited. Still nothing happened. She was about to give up when she got an idea. She began to move Melody's stationery around slowly right next to the bulb.

Now there was a change. It was very faint at first, but she was sure she saw pale brown marks on the paper. And she was sure they were parts of letters!

She moved the paper around some more and looked. More letters came up.

Then there were words!

Veronica tried to read the message, but she couldn't. This time she knew at once why she couldn't read it.

Mirror writing! Veronica thought Melody Hicks was the cleverest girl in the whole world. "A code on top of a code!" Veronica whispered. "I love that Melody!"

Quickly she replaced the lamp shade and went into her room. She closed the door. Then she went to the mirror and held the paper in front of her. Now she could read the message in the mirror:

I never heard of a Polly Winkler Fan Club.
It sounds dumb. Polly Winkler is dumb too.
I have read much better books in my life.

87

Veronica read the message a few times. Then she read it out loud in her sweetest voice. It still didn't sound very friendly.

Why had Melody gone to so much trouble to write a note like that?

A *mystery!* Veronica tucked the note under her pillow. *A real live mystery!*

A Plan
❧ of Attack

The day after Christmas, Veronica's mother went away on a skiing trip. She left Veronica with a new baby-sitter, a lady named Mrs. Moore. Veronica's mother had been pleased to find Mrs. Moore because Mrs. Moore did housework, too. But Veronica never saw Mrs. Moore do anything but watch television—all day and most of the night.

Sometimes, when Veronica felt bored, she started to dial Melody's number, but she hung up before she finished dialing. She didn't know what she would say to Melody. She needed more time to think about it.

Veronica went across the hall a few times to visit Chris. She had to tell him how many Christmas presents she had gotten and how much they probably cost. Then she had to tell him how she almost went skiing, but her mother was afraid she would break her leg.

On New Year's Day, Veronica stopped by to let Chris know how late she had stayed up on New Year's Eve. Later the same day, Veronica brought her cat Gulliver over to play with Chris's cat Tiger.

"Gulliver was feeling lonely," Veronica told Chris.

"Are you staying, too?" Chris asked her.

"Yes," said Veronica.

Later that afternoon Veronica took her poodle out for a walk. It was then that she thought of a plan to meet Melody.

As soon as she got home, she called Hilary's mother. She asked Hilary's mother if she could borrow Wolf.

"I want to take him for a walk tomorrow morning," Veronica said. "I thought he might be lonely with Hilary away."

"Well, isn't that nice," said Hilary's mother. "And how are you, Veronica?"

"Fine," said Veronica. "Well, bye," she said.

Veronica took a few deep breaths. Then she dialed Melody's number.

"Hello?" someone said.

Veronica tried to talk with an English accent.

"May I please talk to Melody Hicks, if you don't mind," she said.

"This is Melody Hicks," said the voice.

"Are you *kidding?*" Veronica shrieked. "Is this really Melody Hicks?"

"Who is this?" The girl sounded suspicious.

"Well, this happens to be Jane . . . Jane Moore," Veronica said in her English accent. "My mother told me to call you. She saw this sign you put up at the library. You see, we have this dog—"

"Oh," said Melody. "I am very experienced with dogs. What kind of dog do you have?"

"Well, I can't really discuss that over the phone," said Veronica.

"Don't worry," said Melody. "I am particularly good with mutts. As a matter of fact, mutts are my specialty."

Veronica almost told Melody right then that she had a poddle with pedigree papers a mile long, but she stopped herself just in time. She had decided to use Wolf because Wolf would scare the life out of Melody.

"By the way," said Melody. "I charge a dollar a walk. But if that is too much, I can make an exception."

"A dollar a walk sounds reasonable," said Veronica. "But my mother wants me to set up an interview first."

"An interview with your dog?" asked Melody.

"Yes, you see, our dog is very fussy," Veronica explained. "We have a very sensitive dog."

"I understand," said Melody. "Many of my clients are sensitive dogs."

Veronica was impressed. Melody sounded so grown-up. She sounded so businesslike.

"Look, Jane," said Melody. "If you want, I can come over right now. Where do you live?"

"Oh, wait a minute," said Veronica. "I just remembered something. You see, our dog happens to be away—for the holidays, you know—he won't be back until late tonight. That is the reason I was wondering if you could meet us tomorrow in front of the library."

There was a silence. Veronica waited for Melody to say something. She suddenly felt very nervous.

"Is this for real?" Melody finally asked.

"Oh, yes, definitely," said Veronica.

"Look, Jane," said Melody. "The only reason I asked that is because some kid went and messed up my sign on the bulletin board."

"How awful!" Veronica squeaked. "Who would do a thing like that?"

"I don't know," said Melody. "But don't worry, I'll find out."

Veronica was so scared she almost hung up, but then she heard Melody ask, "What time? What time do you want me to meet you?"

"Ten o'clock," said Veronica.

"Okay," said Melody. "See you at the library."

The Interview 🐾

It was very cold the next morning. Veronica was glad she was wearing a very warm disguise.

She had on her mother's big white fur hat and a white scarf she had wrapped around her neck a few times. She was also wearing dark glasses.

Veronica carried her father's old briefcase. In the briefcase was a three-page questionnaire for Melody. Veronica had spent hours typing it.

When Veronica went to pick up Wolf, Samantha met her at the door.

"Oh, Mama," Samantha called. "Come see how cute Veronica looks."

"This is what I wear to walk dogs," Veronica explained.

Veronica and Wolf got to the library a few minutes early.

"Good little doggie." Wolf sat down next to

Veronica on the library steps. For some reason Wolf wasn't looking so scary this morning.

Veronica took off one of her mittens and felt in her father's briefcase to make sure the questionnaire was still there.

"Excuse me, miss." A man was standing in front of her. "Isn't the library supposed to be open today?"

Veronica nodded. She knew the library was open for the whole vacation.

"Well, the door is still locked," the man said. "It must be opening late." He went away.

Then Veronica saw a skinny boy coming up the steps. He was wearing an army jacket, blue jeans, and cowboy boots. He had on a light blue knitted hat. The boy came right up to Veronica. "Hi, Jane."

It was a girl's voice. It was Melody's voice. Veronica sat up straight.

"I'm Melody," she said. "You're Jane, right?"

Veronica nodded. She took off her dark glasses so she could see what Melody Hicks looked like.

Melody had a small turned-up nose and freckles all over her face. She had dark blue eyes and long dark lashes. Her cheeks were bright pink from the cold. *Pretty, but tough*, Veronica thought.

"Neat dog," said Melody. "Part wolf, right?" And she sat down next to Veronica.

Melody stuck her hands into the pockets of her army jacket. (*She doesn't even wear mittens!* Veronica thought.) Melody stretched her legs and looked at Veronica.

"Well, can we start now?" she asked.

Veronica nodded. Without a word, she reached into her briefcase and took out the questionnaire. She handed it to Melody.

"What's this?" Melody asked. She read the first line, "JOB INTERVIEW—FILL IN THE ANSWERS." Melody looked at Veronica. "Your mother wrote this?" she asked.

Veronica nodded again.

"Nice Wolfie," Veronica kept saying.

"I never had to fill out one of these before," said Melody, but she reached into a pocket and pulled out a pencil. She read the first question. Veronica peeked over her shoulder.

HOW MANY DOGS HAVE YOU WALKED IN YOUR LIFE? _____

LIST DOGS BY NAME: _____

Melody put the questionnaire on the step above her and started writing. Veronica watched her. Melody wrote very fast.

Veronica put her dark glasses on. She leaned back on the library step. She could hardly believe she was sitting there with Melody Hicks. Wait until she told Hilary!

Melody stopped writing. She seemed puzzled. "My philosophy of dogs?" she mumbled. " 'What is my philosophy of dogs?' . . . Oh, I think I know what she means." Melody started scribbling again.

A few minutes later, Melody poked Veronica. "Hey, Jane," she said. "What does your mother have to know this for?" She showed Veronica the question, ARE YOUR PARENTS MARRIED OR DIVORCED?

Veronica read the question over and over, as if she were seeing it for the first time.

"Don't know," Veronica murmured.

"Oh, well, I guess she has some reason," said Melody, and she circled DIVORCED.

"Mine are, too," Veronica whispered. She felt very happy. She was sure that, somehow, she and Melody were going to be friends. "My parents are divorced, too," she said.

"Oh, yeah?" Melody didn't look up. She was reading the next question.

"Hey!" Melody sounded angry. "Now hold on!" She stuck the paper in Veronica's face. "Just look at this. Now your mother wants to know how many friends I have. That's none of her business."

"Of course not," Veronica said quickly. "You don't have to fill in every single thing."

Melody went back to work. She didn't say anything more, so Veronica leaned back and relaxed. *Things are going well,* she thought.

Wolf stood up. He came over to Veronica and sniffed one of her mittens. Veronica petted him very carefully. Wolf sniffed her other mitten.

"That's not your dog. I can tell," said Melody in a very low voice.

Veronica's mouth dropped open. She stared at Melody. She thought Melody was the sharpest kid she had ever met.

"Wow!" said Veronica. "I don't believe it. You really are an expert on dogs. I thought when you said 'expert' you were just showing off."

"Yeah, but I spelled 'expert' wrong—didn't I?" Melody was studying Veronica's face.

"Oh, don't let that bother you," said Veronica.

"I wasn't even sure of the right spelling myself."

It was only then that Veronica realized she was in trouble. She stood up. "Well, I guess I'd better be going along," she said.

Melody stood up, too. She grabbed Veronica's arm and pushed her back onto the library steps.

"Sit down," said Melody. "You're not going any-place. You're staying right here until this library opens. I'm telling Miss Markham what you did. Wait until she hears who messed up my sign."

For a long time the two girls sat on the library steps. Veronica was so cold she was shivering. Melody looked cold, too, but she just sat there stiffly, her hands in her pockets.

Veronica looked at her watch. It was almost eleven and the library still wasn't open.

Melody looked at her watch, too. Suddenly she stood up and started down the steps.

"Hey!" Veronica called. "Where are you going?"

Melody didn't look back.

"Wait!" Veronica shouted.

At that very moment Veronica realized she would much rather be held prisoner on the library steps than at home watching today's episode of

Twilight of Darkness with Mrs. Moore. She grabbed the briefcase and dragged Wolf down the steps.

Veronica ran after Melody. "But you can't leave!" she called out desperately. "You have to tell Miss Markham on me."

Melody didn't even turn around. She kept walking.

"Hey, Melody. I'll lend you my mittens. You can have my scarf, too," said Veronica. "Please wait, Melody. I have something important to tell you . . ." Veronica put her hand on Melody's arm. Melody shook it off and kept walking.

"Melody, Melody!" Veronica had to run to keep up. "Guess who I am. Guess who I really am!"

Melody stopped. She turned around and faced Veronica.

"I'm the one!" said Veronica. "I'm the one who sent you the get-well card!"

"I should have known," said Melody, and she walked away.

"Oh, Melody," Veronica called. "I think Polly Winkler is dumb, too. I've completely outgrown Polly Winkler."

But Melody wasn't interested. She was heading

toward a coffee shop at the end of the block. She pulled open the door.

"MELODY!" Veronica screamed. "I ONLY WANTED TO MEET YOU. I DID IT BECAUSE I WANTED TO MEET YOU!"

Melody gave Veronica a strange look and disappeared into the coffee shop.

Veronica stood on the sidewalk a few seconds. Then she tied Wolf's leash to a parking meter and followed Melody into the coffee shop.

"Excuse me, mister." Melody was talking to the man behind the counter. "Do you know why the library isn't open yet?"

"Budget cuts," said the man. "It's not going to open."

"You mean it's closed for good?"

"Looks that way," said the man.

"But they can't *do* that!" Veronica shouted.

Melody turned and looked at Veronica.

"You're telling me," she said.

"You can take your books across town to the St. Nicholas branch," the man said.

"But there's no children's room there," said Melody.

Veronica was now standing right next to Melody. "If you ask me," she said, "they all hate kids."

"Everyone hates kids," Melody agreed.

"Can I get you girls anything?" the man asked.

Melody reached into her pocket. Her hands were red and chapped. She took out some change and counted it.

"A cup of hot chocolate, please," she said.

Then Melody looked at Veronica. Veronica's nose was bright red. Her teeth were chattering.

"Mister," said Melody. "Could I have that hot chocolate with two cups, please?"

Hot Chocolate
❧ for Two

The man in the coffee shop was very nice. He let Melody and Veronica sit at a table near the window so that Veronica could keep an eye on Wolf.

And as soon as they finished their half-cups of hot chocolate, he filled their cups up again.

"But I can't pay for this," said Melody. "I don't have any more money."

"On the house," the man said. He turned to a man sitting at the next table. "It's all in a good cause," he said, and he winked at the other man.

Veronica and Melody were working hard. They were trying to write a letter to the mayor about the closing of the library. Veronica and Melody were writing ideas on paper napkins.

"How's this?" asked Melody. She picked up her napkin and read: "Dear Mr. Mayor, You aren't fooling us. We know you take the tax money and spend it on fancy cars and restaurants. . . ."

Melody stopped. She read it over to herself.

"No . . ." she said. "That's no good. What do you have?" she asked Veronica.

Veronica read from her napkin: "Dear Mr. Mayor, You think you are so big. Now that the Harding Branch of the library is closed, I'll bet that makes you happy. I'll bet it makes you happy because you don't care a thing about kids. You don't care about kids because you know they can't vote for you."

The man at the next table started coughing.

Veronica and Melody turned around and looked at him.

"He's laughing," Veronica whispered.

"He's laughing at us!" Melody was furious.

"Girls," said the man, "I'm sorry for eavesdropping. I think you are doing a wonderful thing, but do you mind if I make a suggestion?"

The two girls looked away. They didn't answer him.

"Look," he said. "I work for a newspaper. I'm a reporter for the *Daily Times*."

Veronica's eyes opened wide. Melody turned and stared at the man. A real live reporter was talking to them!

"Girls," he said. "Did you ever think of writing to a newspaper? You know they publish a column called 'Letters to the Editor.' Lots of people read those letters."

"Us?" Veronica asked. "You mean they might put our names in a newspaper?"

"Who knows?" The man was smiling at them.

"Let's try," Melody whispered.

The two girls went back to work.

After quite a long time, Melody said, "Okay, what do you think of this?"

"Dear Editor, No one should be allowed to close a library. If people used the library more often, they wouldn't be so stupid. . . ."

"Let me see that," said Veronica, and she took the napkin from Melody. She read it over a few times. She thought very hard about it.

"Melody," she said slowly, "it is good. It is very very good, but do you think we could leave out the part . . ."

"What part?" asked Melody.

". . . the part that, well, makes people feel bad," said Veronica.

"But they should feel bad," said Melody. "The library is closed."

"Yes, but look . . ." Veronica was finding it difficult to put what she was thinking into words. "We're making them feel bad for being so stupid. Do you think we could make them feel smart and sad about the library at the same time?"

Melody didn't say anything. *Now she hates me,* Veronica thought. *Now I've gone and hurt her feelings!*

But Melody said, "My mother does that."

"Huh?" Veronica said. "Does what?"

"Well, my mother sells cosmetics from door to door—you know, lipstick and makeup and stuff like that. Well, anyway, she says she has to make people feel smart and bad at the same time."

"Bad because they are ugly, right?" said Veronica.

"No," said Melody. "Not really." She sighed. "Selling cosmetics is very complicated."

"Well, tell me," Veronica begged her. "I'll understand. I promise I'll understand."

"Look," said Melody. She leaned forward across the table. "My mother has to make them think they could be beautiful if they only tried."

106

"Oh," said Veronica. "Well, anyway . . ."

"You'll need this." The reporter was standing next to their table. He placed two pieces of white paper and an envelope on the table.

"What's this for?" asked Melody.

"For your final draft," said the reporter.

"What's that?" Melody asked.

"Well, I hope you're not going to send my newspaper a bunch of napkins," he said.

The two girls giggled.

The reporter handed Veronica a newspaper. "The address is on the editorial page," he said. "Well, girls, good luck! I think you're on to something." And he left the coffee shop.

Veronica and Melody stared at the newspaper.

"I don't believe it!" Melody said. "Do you realize this newspaper came from a real reporter? We've got to keep this newspaper *forever!*"

"Oh, if only we had gotten him to autograph it for us!" said Veronica.

Your Friend, Melody &

They were so excited, it took a few minutes for them to get back to work.

"I think I've got an idea," Veronica said.

"What?" asked Melody.

"I can't talk about it yet," said Veronica. "I've got to write it down first."

She took a clean paper napkin and began to write:

Dear Editor,

We were very sad to hear that the Harding Branch of the library was closed. That one has a children's room that we go to.

Grown-ups are always saying that children watch too much television. Well, what do they expect if we can't even get books out of our library? It's not that we don't like television, but there are some ways that books are better . . .

Veronica took another napkin.

1. There is no laugh track in a book. You can laugh when you feel like it. Also there is no music during the sad parts trying to make you cry. Some people laugh at the sad parts and cry at the happy parts. They have a right, it is a free country.

Veronica thought for a few seconds. Melody handed her another napkin. Veronica began writing again:

2. You can choose from a million books and then you can read them whenever you feel like it. You don't have to wait for some program to come on television. And besides, everyone knows that grown-ups put the best programs on when children are asleep in bed. This is done on purpose.

"Read it! Read it!" Melody was very excited.

"I don't think I'm finished," said Veronica.

"Well, then, read what you have!" said Melody impatiently.

Veronica read what she had.

"Yup," said Melody. "We'll definitely write that."

"But I need a Number 3. I need another good reason," said Veronica.

"Why?" Melody asked.

"I don't know," said Veronica. "I just do."

"Maybe I can think of one." Melody began chewing on her pencil.

But it was Veronica who began writing again.

"Listen," said Veronica. "Number 3. They teach you to read at school. They do not teach you to watch TV. Therefore, books must be more educational—"

"That's boring," said Melody.

"You're right," said Veronica. "Besides, if we say a lot of mean things about television, they might take it away."

"Wait a minute!" Melody began scribbling. "Listen," she said. Melody took a deep breath and read: "Number 3. It is easier to read a book under the covers as long as you have a good flashlight. A television would make a big lump in your bed. Then you would be caught and probably punished—"

"No!" Veronica was horrified. "We can't write that. If grown-ups ever found out that kids did that, they would be happy when all the books disappeared from the world. They would be dancing all over the place."

"Well, I tried," said Melody sadly. "We'll just have to end with Number 2."

Veronica was disappointed. It didn't feel right.

"Unless . . ." Melody said, "unless you want to talk about how you can't look things up on television."

"Huh?" Veronica asked.

"Well," said Melody. "You see, I'm always asking my mother these questions and she's so busy she doesn't even hear what I say. So I have to look it up in a book."

"Write it!" Veronica shouted.

Melody smiled. She pulled out another napkin and wrote.

Then they laid out the napkins on the table like a jigsaw puzzle. They added a few lines.

"You write the final draft," said Melody. "You have nicer handwriting."

"Thanks," said Veronica. And she began to write—very neatly. When she was finished, they both read the letter over.

"You know," said Melody. "I think we need a last line. Something really POW!"

"You're right," said Veronica. "How about 'Please save the library'?"

"No!" Melody shouted. "Definitely no! Why should we say 'Please' to a bunch of dumb grown-ups? They use the library, too. We're not the only ones. Come on," she said to Veronica. *"Think!"*

They both thought. The man came over and filled up their cups with hot chocolate. He did it very carefully so he would not disturb any of the napkins lying on the table.

No one said anything for a long time.

"Veronica," Melody whispered, "I just thought of something."

"What?" Veronica asked.

"It's really creepy," said Melody. "No, I can't tell you. It's too creepy."

"Tell me! Tell me!" Veronica begged her.

"It gives me the shivers," said Melody.

Veronica couldn't stand it. "You've *got* to tell me," she said.

"Well, all right." Melody leaned across the table. She whispered. "Did you ever feel that books are really *alive*? Not things, you know, but alive?" Melody looked scared, but she went on. "It's almost like books can *breathe*—the way rabbits

112

breathe, or dogs or cats. Do you know what I mean?"

"Well, of course," Veronica said sharply. "More like birds," she added.

Melody looked surprised for a second. Then she whispered, "Well, then, just think of them—just think of them lying there in that library!"

"I'm writing that," said Veronica. She didn't bother to take another napkin. She wrote right on the final draft.

"Writing what?" Melody asked.

But Veronica didn't really know. She just wrote.

When she finished, she read it over. She was sorry she hadn't written on a napkin first.

"Oh, no!" Veronica wailed. "Oh, no! Now look what I've done. I've ruined the whole letter!" She felt like crying.

"Let me see it." Melody took the letter and read it.

This is what Veronica had written:

It makes us sick to think of all those books locked up in our library, trying to get out. Not only that. Who will take care of them?

"You dumbbell," said Melody when she had finished reading. "There's nothing wrong with that. It's true. It's really true!"

Veronica stared at Melody. Melody looked angry.

"It's absolutely true!" Melody said. "You didn't ruin anything."

"I didn't?" Veronica asked in a very small voice.

"No," said Melody. "Now sign your name."

Veronica signed her name. She passed the letter to Melody to sign. "Your turn," she said.

But Melody wouldn't sign. "You wrote most of it," she said. "You should get the credit."

"No!" said Veronica. "We *both* wrote it. You thought of the best parts."

Melody began to fold the letter.

"Wait!" Veronica tried to take the letter back. "I'm going to write a little P.S. about how you helped." Melody stuck the letter in the envelope and began to seal it.

"But I love P.S.'s!" said Veronica.

"I know," said Melody. "I've seen some of your little P.S.'s." She waved the letter in the air. "Too late!" Melody grinned.

"Oh, well" said Veronica, "they'll never print it

anyway." Melody was helping her walk Wolf back to Hilary's house.

"Then we'll write another one," said Melody.

". . . and another," said Veronica, "and another, until they open the library again."

"Oh, boy, I just got an idea for the next letter," said Melody. "We could end like this: 'And if it weren't for the library, we would never have met and become friends.' "

Friends? Veronica couldn't believe her ears. *Me, Veronica, with two friends?* She stared at Melody.

Melody was embarrassed. "I just thought it sounded good," she said.

"It sounds very good," said Veronica.

The End of Vacation 🐾

On the first day of school, Veronica overslept. She missed the bus Hilary usually took to school. She had to wait for another one.

Hilary was waiting on the school steps.

"Veronica!" Hilary ran to meet her. "Veronica! You've got to tell me what happened. My mother said that Melody Hicks was at my house—that she was sitting right in my living room! And I had to be away! Oh, Veronica, how did it happen?"

"Melody helped me walk Wolf home," said Veronica. "Did you have fun? What did you do at your cousin's house?"

"Things," said Hilary. "Come on, Veronica! Tell me right now how it happened. How did you meet her?"

The late bell rang. Veronica grabbed Hilary's hand. "I promise I'll tell you the whole story later. Besides, we have a date with Melody this afternoon, so you'll meet her in person."

116

"A DATE WITH MELODY HICKS?" Hilary was so stunned, Veronica had to pull her in the door.

When they got to their classroom, the seats were all empty. Veronica and Hilary looked around. Everyone was standing around the bulletin board looking at something.

The first thing Veronica noticed was Amy's face. Amy looked angry. When Amy saw Veronica, she said, "Here she is. Big deal!"

But when the teacher saw Veronica, she smiled. She seemed very excited.

"Well, congratulations, Veronica. You did a wonderful job. I guess you must feel like quite a hero today."

Veronica couldn't figure out what the teacher was talking about.

Hilary went to the bulletin board. "Veronica!" she yelled. "A letter you wrote is in the newspaper. And you didn't even tell me!"

"I didn't even know," Veronica whispered. She dropped her books on top of a desk.

Suddenly Veronica felt very weak. She sat down and crossed her arms on the desk. She hid her face in her arms. Her face felt hot.

A few kids came over and said things like,

117

"Congratulations!" "Terrific!" and "Good letter!" Veronica just nodded with her head still in her arms. She wondered if she were sick.

"Are you all right, Veronica?" the teacher asked.

Veronica looked up. "I feel a little funny," she said. "I guess I'm just surprised."

Then she noticed that Kimberly was reading the letter. Amy was trying to pull Kimberly away from the bulletin board.

"Don't read it," Amy said to Kimberly. "You know it's going to be dumb. She only did it to get attention."

"I want to read it," said Kimberly. "My father read it out loud at breakfast, but I didn't know it was Veronica who wrote it. My father says that sometimes a letter like this can do a lot of good."

"Oh, Kimberly," Amy wailed. "I can't stand it. That Veronica is already such a show-off. She thinks she's so great. Look at her. Just look at her showing off!"

Kimberly turned around and looked at Veronica.

Veronica was still sitting at the desk. She seemed to be in a daze. Hilary was standing silently by—holding Veronica's hand.

Kimberly said softly, "She doesn't look like she's showing off."

"Well, she's just pretending. Right this minute she's acting real shy and modest, but wait—just wait. Now she'll never stop. She'll just get worse and worse."

"Maybe," said Kimberly. "But it *is* a good letter." And she read it again.

PROTEST THE LIBRARY CLOSING

Dear Editor,

We were very sad to hear that the Harding Branch of the library was closed. That one has a children's room that we go to.

Grown-ups are always saying that children watch too much television. Well, what do they expect if we can't even get books out of our library? It's not that we don't like television, but there are some ways that books are better.

1. There is no laugh track in a book. You can laugh when you feel like it. Also there is no music during the sad parts trying to make you cry. Some people laugh at the sad parts and cry at the happy parts. They have a right, it is a free country.

2. You can choose from a million books and then you can read them whenever you feel like it. You can read your favorite part over and over. You don't have to wait for some program to come on television. And, besides, everyone knows that grown-ups put the best programs on television when children are in bed asleep. This is done on purpose.

3. What if you have to find out something in a hurry and what if no one knew the answer or was too busy and what if it was a matter of life and death? You could look it up in a book. Not to mention how much fun it is to read along the library shelves. Sometimes you find a book about things you never even heard of.

It makes us sick to think of all those books locked up in our library, trying to get out. Not only that. Who will take care of them?

Your friend,
VERONICA SCHMIDT

119